This book belongs to:

I ♥ DAD

FOR DAD'S FAVOURITE COOKIES

- flour
- chocolate
- eggs
- butter
- more chocolate
- sprinkles

DAD KEEP OUT!

ONE CLEAN ROOM COUPON.

Presents for DAD

- Drill
- Ball
- Hat and Scarf
- Hair gel
- Play day

LEAF FOR DAD

DAD + MUM = ME

TOP-SECRET!

How to Surprise a DAD

by JEAN REAGAN

illustrated by LEE WILDISH

h

Hodder
Children's
Books

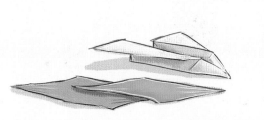

for John and Jane's dad
(SURPRISE!) —J.R.

Ivy, you surprise me all the time.
Love, Dad —L.W.

First published in the United States by Alfred A. Knopf, an imprint of
Random House Children's Books, a division of Random House, Inc., New York.

This paperback edition first published in the UK in 2016 by Hodder Children's Books.

Hodder Children's Books
An imprint of Hachette Children's Group
Part of Hodder & Stoughton
Carmelite House, 50 Victoria Embankment,
London EC4Y 0DZ

A catalogue record of this book is available from the British Library.

ISBN: 978 1 444 92467 1

10 9 8 7 6 5 4 3 2 1

An Hachette UK Company
www.hachette.co.uk

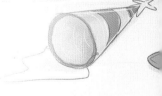

Shhhhhhh!
To surprise a dad, you have to be tricky.

First of all, don't let him
see this book.

HOW TO HIDE THIS BOOK:

Wrap it in paper and cover it
with pictures. (That way, he'll
never know it's about him.)

Tuck it between boring
books no one ever reads.

Where's the *polka-dot hippo* book?
Wink, wink

Make up a secret name for it,
like — *polka-dot hippo*. (Be sure
to wink when you say it.)

You may already be good at surprises, but do you want to become a *super dad-surpriser*? Great!

Luckily, *any* day is a perfect day to surprise a dad, and there are so many different ways.

Some surprises you MAKE:

Draw hearts and stick them everywhere.

Build a snow-dad.

Invent something amazing,
just for him.

Other surprises you **DO**:

Get his toothbrush ready.

Reorganise his shoes and hats.

Help him with the
supermarket shopping.

If you want to
make him laugh,
walk and talk
like a dad.

Some surprises you don't *make* or *do*.
Instead, you. . .

...FIND them.

HOW TO FIND SURPRISES:

Look up, down, under and all around.

Stay perfectly still and listen.

Dig a hole, sift through
sand or kick up leaves.

Kids have good eyes for nature (dads, not so much).
So surprise him when you find:

A caterpillar nibbling on a leaf. A squirrel hiding in a tree.

Dandelions for a bouquet. A heart-shaped rock.

A busy, busy anthill. Geese flying high above.

Now that you're an expert on *any* day surprises,
you are ready for. . . Special Day surprises!

These take a little more planning. (If your mum
is good at keeping secrets, ask her to help.)

SPECIAL DAYS FOR DADS:

His birthday

Father's Day

Congratulations

Welcome Home

CALENDAR

First, choose when to have the big surprise,
and decide who to invite:

Just your family?

Your pets?   Your stuffed animals?

His friends?   Your friends?

Relatives?   Neighbours?

Then, decorate with his favourite colour. Keep it simple or go wild! (Remember to save some ideas for next time.)

Now, plan the yummiest part of the surprise – THE TREATS!

Create a dessert that looks like your dad. Bake cookies with extra chocolate chips.

It's your dad's special day, so be sure to have his favourites:

Spicy crisps
Smoked oysters
Super-stinky cheese

Don't forget presents!

PRESENTS FOR A DAD:

Shirt and tie.
(Instead of wrapping these,
wear them for an even
bigger surprise.)

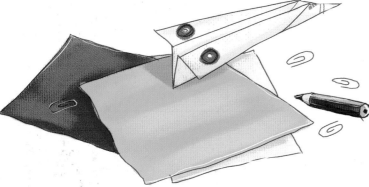

Everything you need
to make paper aeroplanes
together.

A secret treasure
map of your garden.

(Check also: ANY DAY SURPRISES you make, do or find.)

If your dad gets suspicious and asks,

Look innocent.
(Practise this in a mirror.)

Say something like, "It's very boring
behind you. You shouldn't turn around."

Think fast — distract him with
a crazy dance!

When it's surprise time, make sure everyone is hiding.

HOW TO HIDE EVERYONE:

Between the pictures,
plants or balloons.

ORANGEADE

Surprise!

Behind the curtains, sofa or coat rack.

Under the table, cushions or blankets.

While you wait for your dad, practise whispering "Surprise."

OK, now *shhhhhhh*. . .

Remember, of *all* the surprises, the best ones are
the special ones you dream up just for *your* dad.

Now, don't forget to hide this book. And *shhhhhhh!*

If you *do* want to let your dad read it,
have him say this pledge aloud
before he starts:

I ♥ DAD

I, Dad,
promise not to remember
anything in this book.
Especially anything about surprises.

I ♥ DAD

FOR DAD's FAVOURITE COOKIES
- flour
- chocolate
- eggs
- butter
- more chocolate
- sprinkles

DAD KEEP OUT!

ONE CLEAN ROOM COUPON.

Presents for DAD
- Drill
- Ball
- Hat and Scarf
- Hair gel
- Play day

LEAF FOR DAD

DAD + MUM = ME

TOP-SECRET!

From the author-illustrator team behind
the bestselling *How to Babysit* series:

For fun activities, further information and to order,
visit www.hodderchildrens.co.uk